Jack and the Beanstalk

Nina Crews

Christy Ottaviano Books

Henry Holt and Company

New York

Thank-you to Benjamin Chang, who starred as Jack.
Thank-you to Sam Henriques, Juliette Hewitt, and Damian
Gerndt, who starred as the giant, his wife, and Mrs. M.
Also thanks to Wilma McDaniel, Anne Kobayashi,
Hiroshi Tamada, Margot Hughes, and Ben Stein,
for their assistance on this project.

Henry Holt and Company, LLC
Publishers since 1866
175 Fifth Avenue
New York, New York 10010
mackids.com

Henry Holt® is a registered trademark of Henry Holt and Company, LLC.
Copyright © 2011 by Nina Crews
All rights reserved.

Library of Congress Cataloging-in-Publication Data
Crews, Nina.
Jack and the beanstalk / by Nina Crews. — 1st ed.
p.   cm.
"Christy Ottaviano Books."
Summary: Photo-collage illustrations and updated text provide a new look at the traditional tale
of a boy who plants magic beans, climbs the beanstalk, and is captured by a giant and his wife.
ISBN 978-0-8050-8765-9
[1. Fairy tales. 2. Giants—Folklore. 3. Folklore—England.] I. Title.
PZ8.C866Jac 2011
398.2—dc20
[E]
2010026951

First Edition—2011

The artist used Adobe® Photoshop® to color-correct and manipulate 35-mm digital
photographs and line drawings to create the illustrations for this book.

Printed in April 2011 in Singapore by Imago

1 3 5 7 9 10 8 6 4 2

To Edward

When Jack came home from his first day of work doing chores for his neighbor Mrs. M, he was disappointed. She had given him multicolored beans instead of money.

"These are worth more than what I owe you," she said. "Make sure you plant them right away."

Jack wasn't certain he believed her, but he went ahead and planted the beans outside his bedroom window.

next morning, Jack overslept.
parents had to wake him up.

room was unusually dark.
looked out the window.

razy!

s a beanstalk!"

started to suspect that something
derful was happening.

The beanstalk grew and grew, looping and twisting its way up into the sky. By noon, the beanstalk was taller than the house. Jack shook the huge vine. It was very sturdy. Later that afternoon, the beanstalk disappeared into the clouds, and Jack found that it was easy to climb.

Jack climbed. He went farther and farther up the huge beanstalk. When Jack stopped to rest, he was so high he could see the entire city.

"WOW!"

Jack kept climbing. A breeze carried the scent
of freshly baked chocolate chip cookies. "Mmm,"
thought Jack. "It would be nice to have a snack."

He saw a castle. The cookies must be inside.
Jack wouldn't normally go into a stranger's home,
but this wasn't a normal day. So Jack walked in.

Inside was the
biggest
man he'd ever seen.

"You are one lucky woman," said the giant. "I look good.
I smell good. You are married to the biggest, handsomest
man—ever. When they made me, they broke the mold.
Rub some lotion on my feet once you're done there."

The giant kept bragging. Jack tried not to laugh,
but eventually he let out a little giggle.

"What's that noise?"
said the giant.
"What's that smell?

FEE, FIE, FOE, FUM,

I smell me a young 'un!
Looks like your cookies
caught us a new boy!"

"Dear," said the giant's wife,
"try to be gentle with this one.
You don't know your own strength."

"Me?" he said. "I'm a pussycat.
That last boy was worthless.

"I take good care of valuable things," said the giant as he snatched up his hen. "Sweet hen, lay me some eggs!

"You can touch it, boy, but you can't keep it. These are 24-karat, solid gold eggs.

"I bet you wish you had a hen like this. Well, she's the only one and she's mine.

"Wife! Give this boy some chores! There's a lot that needs doing around here, and I need a nap."

The giant's wife took Jack into the kitchen to begin the longest afternoon of his young life. He swept. He scrubbed. He washed. He chopped wood. He shined every knife, fork, and spoon they had. And they had a lot. The work was very hard. The giant snored in the next room.

Jack was hungry and tired. He wanted to go home.

"I need something from the pantry," said the giant's wife. "I'll be right back. Start peeling the carrots."

NOW! As soon as she left the room, Jack ran! He ran past the giant. He ran past the hen, which let out a loud "Squawk!" Jack grabbed it.

"Boy! Boy!" yelled the giant's wife.

Jack ran out of the house with the hen squawking and clucking under his arm.

"My hen!" the giant roared.

Jack started down the vine as fast as he could while holding the hen tightly. He couldn't believe that he'd taken it from right under the giant's nose.

The vine began to shake
as the giant and his wife
climbed down after him.

"STOP!

My hen! My hen!"

the giant shouted again.

The beanstalk swayed back and forth. The giant and his wife were getting closer. Jack leapt to the ground. He got his father's saw and started to cut the thick vine.

Finally, Jack cut the base of the beanstalk deeply enough that it snapped and toppled over. The giant and his wife tumbled down.

whoa!

Jack stood stunned. What had he done? All was still.

A minute passed, and then from under the leaves came a man and a woman who looked very much like the giant and his wife, only smaller.

"There's my hen," said the man.

"Brother!" Mrs. M ran up and gave the man a big hug.

"This boy broke the spell," said the man. "I once wished to be the biggest, richest man there was.

That got me and my wife stuck up in the clouds. We owe you."

"Thank you," said the woman.

"I knew you'd be just the boy for the job," said Mrs. M.

Jack smiled. He was safe and nobody was hurt. But he was still hungry and tired, so he went home.

And in the morning, on his doorstep,

there was a bowl of fresh eggs.